Taking Turns

Written by
Marianne Blackstone Tabner

Illustrated by
Gail M. Nelson

Taking Turns
Published by Star of the Sea Publishing
San Diego, CA

Publisher's Cataloging-in-Publication data

Names: Blackstone Tabner, Marianne, author. Nelson, Gail M., illustrator.
Title: Taking Turns / by Marianne Blackstone Tabner. Illustrated by Gail M. Nelson.
Description: First paperback original edition. | San Diego [California] : Star of the Sea Publishing, 2020. | Also published as hardcover. | Also published in Spanish. | Appendix included.
Summary: Moon's refusal to take turns with Sun not only impacts his friend, but affects the whole planet Earth.
Identifiers: ISBN 978-1-7351483-0-4
Subjects: CYAC: Friendship. | Sharing. | Moon. | Sun.
BISAC: JUVENILE FICTION / Social Themes / Friendship. | JUVENILE FICTION / Science & Nature / General.
Classification: LCC PS490 | DDC 813.6 BLACKSTONE TABNER–dc22

QUANTITY PURCHASES: Schools, companies, clubs, and other organizations may qualify for special terms when ordering quantities of this title. For information, email info@StaroftheSeaPublishing.com.

Printed in the United States of America.

For my granddaughter Kira.
Love you to the Moon and back!

Moon beams all night
Reflecting Sun's light.

Sun shines brightly all day.

Sun and Moon have been
together for a lifetime.

Moon plays with
the stars making
them giggle and wiggle.

Moon makes soft shadows below.

Village is aglow.

Owls screech. Shorebirds peep.

Moon is in charge.

Moon illuminates night's darkness.

Sun creates day's light.

Rise and shine!

Village comes alive.

Sun is
so happy.

Children hurry to school.
People go to work.

Animals and children play.
Flowers grow and bloom.

Until one evening, Moon
stays out all night,
AND all day.

Moon wants all the
attention.
Moon is showing Sun
who is wiser.

The next morning, Sun
pushed so hard to rise.

Sun pushed and pushed
and could not rise.

Moon refused to share
the sky.

It stayed dark
ALL day and night.

Village didn't go to school.
Village didn't go to work.

Flowers never bloomed.
Village was confused.

Sun missed Village.

Sun began to cry,
and cry...

Sun's tears created a big storm.

Clouds turned gray and dark.

The ocean became bigger and bigger.

Thunder rumbled in
with lightning and said,

"You are equally special.
Sometimes we need Moon
and sometimes we need Sun.

How can you work this out?"

Sun said, "Moon, Village needs you to calm the ocean tides, reflect my light in the darkness for Village to sleep.

Village loves watching you and the stars play at night."

Moon smiled with pride.

Moon was so happy to hear that
Village loves watching Moon.

Sun said, "We ARE both special Moon.
Can we take turns like we always have?"

The next day, Sun took its turn.

Rise and Shine!

Village children laughed and played with the animals.

Flowers danced and bloomed.

Village was so happy to see Sun again.

Then Moon took its turn,
beaming like a flashlight
high in the sky.

Village watched Moon
play with the stars again.

Village was so happy.

Children skipped in the streets
and played in Moon's shadow.

Owls screeched.
Shorebirds peeped.

Moon is at peace.
Village is asleep.

Sun and Moon asked Earth to help them Explain who is really Taking Turns

Q: What two objects have the biggest impact on Earth?

A: Sun and Moon.

Q: Sun, how far are you really from Earth?

A: I am a gigantic ball of hot gas, 150 million kilometers (about 93 million miles) away from Earth. I am at the center of the Solar System.

Q: Sun, do you rotate around the Earth?

A: No, I do not rotate around you, Planet Earth, you rotate around me. You rotate on your own axis every 24 hours, establishing the daily rhythm of Sun rising in the East in the morning and setting in the West in the evening. It takes an entire year for Planet Earth to complete an orbit around Sun.

Q: Moon, how far are you from our Planet Earth?

A: I am much closer to you, Planet Earth, than Sun. Moon is almost 400,000 kilometers away, (about 248,000 miles) and rotates around you, Planet Earth, roughly once every 30 days, giving you your monthly cycle through the year.

Q: Who creates light?

A: Sun is the only object in the Solar System that creates light. Moon reflects the light of Sun back to us on Planet Earth.

Q: Why does Moon's shape seem to change?

A: Moon always shows us the same face, but depending upon where Sun, Moon and Earth are in relation to one another, Moon appears to change its shape throughout the month—from a slender crescent at the start of the month (a New Moon) to a beautiful circular disc in the middle of the month (a Full Moon). This is because Moon itself does not generate its own light.

Q: What creates the tides of the ocean?

A: Tides are actually waves. They are the biggest waves on the planet, and cause the sea to rise and fall along the shore all around the world. Tides are created by the gravitational pull of Moon and Sun but vary depending on where Moon and Sun are in relation to the ocean as you, Planet Earth, rotate on your own axis.

Q: How are day and night created?

A: The daily rotation of your own axis, Planet Earth, gives us the experience of day and night—day when our side of the planet is facing Sun and night when our side of the planet is facing away from Sun. It is easiest to see Moon in the sky at night when the sky is dark. So...It appears to us that Sun and Moon are "Taking Turns" in the sky—Sun during the daytime and Moon during the nighttime!

Visit "Mimi's Story Hour" at
MarianneBlackstoneTabner.com
for additional resources and hands on activities for
teachers and parents to help children learn.

Sources

Fairclough, Caty. Nov. 2013 Smithsonian Ocean find your blue.
https://ocean.si.edu/planet-ocean/tides-currents/currents-waves-and-tides-ocean-motion#:~:text=Tides%20are%20actually%20waves%2C%20the,earth%20rotates%20on%20its%20axis.

Standish, Myles. Earthsky. June 26, 2013. https://earthsky.org/space/coincidence-that-sun-and-moon-seem-same-size

https://solarsystem.nasa.gov/planets/earth/overview/. NASA.gov.
Page Updated: March 22, 2019.

https://solarsystem.nasa.gov/solar-system/sun/overview/. NASA.Gov.
Page Updated: October 2, 2019

About the Author

Marianne Blackstone Tabner is passionately curious about everything. As an author, she shares her own fascination of learning with children by making reading fun. Taking Turns, offered in both English and Spanish, helps children to explore concepts of sharing while providing them with opportunities to expand their creativity and imagination with hands-on science activities.

Inspired by the birth of her first grandchild, Marianne rediscovered her passion to advocate for children's literacy and their learning needs which began when she was a special education teacher in the Boston suburbs.

Marianne is a devoted supporter of local and national literacy foundations. A portion of Marianne's proceeds is donated to "Every Child a Reader" and "Children's Literacy Foundation (Clif)."

Marianne has created "Mimi's Story Hour" to share her love of reading with children and to provide fun, educational, hands-on activities for parents and teachers. Visit MarianneBlackstoneTabner.com to access more resources and to follow "Mimi" on her next story hour adventure.

She now lives, writes, and plays in sunny San Diego, CA.

About the Illustrator

Gail M. Nelson is passionate about books—she loves to design books, illustrate children's books, and read books for her many book clubs. She has a Master's degree in fine art and she has been a freelance artist, illustrator and designer for over thirty years.

Gail enjoys watching Sun, Moon and the stars in the sky over her home in the mountains of Colorado where she lives with her husband and their dog, Luna.

Made in the USA
Coppell, TX
08 November 2020